A VISIT TO THE ZOO

Elisabeth "Lizzy" Katherine Reaves

Illustrated by Harry James, Jr.

AuthorHouse™
1663 Liberty Drive
Bloomington, IN 47403
www.authorhouse.com
Phone: 833-262-8899

This book is printed on acid-free paper.

ISBN: 978-1-6655-3123-8 (sc)
ISBN: 978-1-6655-3122-1 (e)

Library of Congress Control Number: 2021913680

Print information available on the last page.

Published by AuthorHouse 07/14/2021

authorHOUSE®

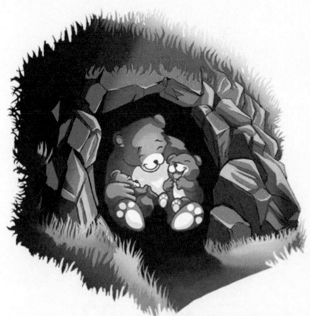

YOU CAN SEE THE BEARS

LIONS

TIGERS

AND ELEPHANTS

YOU CAN SEE THE MONKEYS EATING THEIR BANANAS!

GORILLAS IN THE TREE...

YOU CAN SEE THE BIG HIPPOPOTAMUS

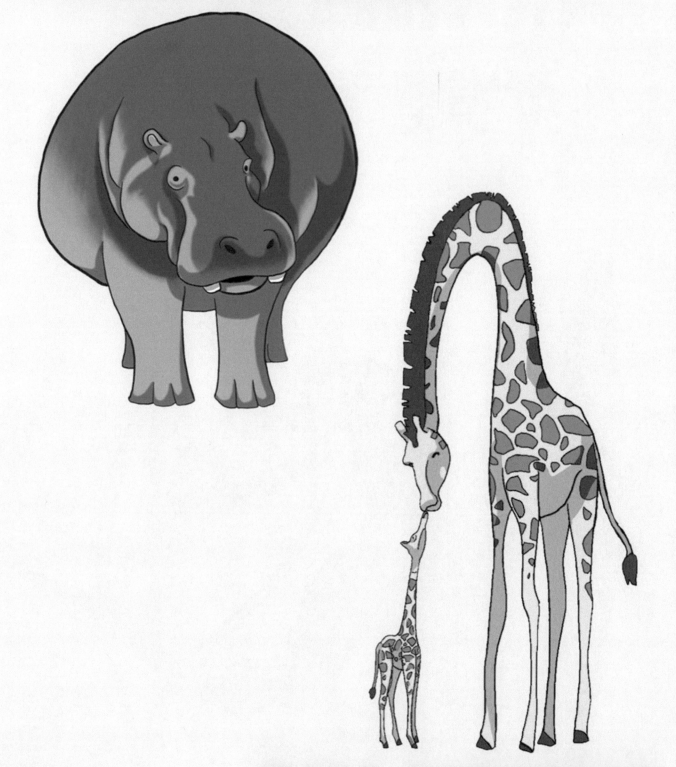

TALL GIRAFFES

THE STRIPED ZEBRAS WHO CAN RUN SO FAST

THE BABY BIRDS
IN THE NEST
WITH THEIR MOMMY

THE PANDA EATING BAMBO

OH LOOK AT ALL OF THOSE FISHES, THEY ARE BEAUTIFUL!

WOW! LOOK AT THE WHALE. IT'S HUGE!

A FAMILY OF PENQUINS

EVEN THE COLORFUL PEACOCK

YOU CAN WALK

BABIES CAN RIDE IN STOLLERS

YOU CAN TAKE THE TRAIN TO THE ZOO

COME WITH US, BECAUSE WE LOVE THE ZOO!

THE END.

Printed in the United States
by Baker & Taylor Publisher Services